I0520036

John:

His Gospel

and

the Revelation

A Novel

Leonard W. Mann

CSS Publishing Company, Inc.
Lima, Ohio

FIRST EDITION
Copyright © 2015
by CSS Publishing Co., Inc.

Published by CSS Publishing Company, Inc., Lima, Ohio 45807. All rights reserved. No part of this publication may be reproduced in any manner whatsoever without the prior permission of the publisher, except in the case of brief quotations embodied in critical articles and reviews. Inquiries should be addressed to: CSS Publishing Company, Inc., Permissions Department, 5450 N. Dixie Highway, Lima, Ohio 45807.

Library of Congress Cataloging-in-Publication Data

For more information about CSS Publishing Company resources, visit our website at www.csspub.com, email us at csr@csspub.com, or call (800) 241-4056.

e-book:
ISBN-13: 978-0-7880-2830-4
ISBN-10: 0-7880-2830-8

ISBN-13: 978-0-7880-2829-8
ISBN-10: 0-7880-2829-4   PRINTED IN USA

Introduction

When appointing his twelve, what qualifications did Jesus look for in the men he chose? We will never know. But we do know this: Most were neighbors, friends, and family. Two of the kin were his first cousins, James and John, brothers, sons of his mother's sister.

John, years younger than Jesus, probably looked with unabashed admiration upon this alluring older cousin. When Jesus invited John to follow him, it was with alacrity that John accepted his cousin's call. Adoringly, he followed — closely. For three or more years he followed, his fine young mind ever alert, his well-tuned spirit playing at crescendo.

Then came that day at Mount Calvary, and John was there, only he from among the twelve. His aunt Mary, the mother of Jesus, was there too, her trembling body sustained, I think, by John's young right arm.

From the place of his dying, Jesus addressed none of the others standing by, but he spoke to these two: "Woman, behold your son; son, behold your mother." Jesus gave to his cousin the lifetime care of his mother. Yes, he might have chosen a stepson of Mary, one of Joseph's children perhaps, but he did not; he chose John. Many years afterward, John would write of himself as "a disciple whom Jesus loved." Clearly, he was.

As the distraught and bewildered disciples left the hilltop that day, it is easy to visualize a frail elderly woman leaning heavily upon a strong young man. These two would go down together into Jerusalem's people's places, and there soon disappear.

Yes, in the scriptural record we will see John three sunrisings afterward, as he outruns Simon Peter in a race to the emptied tomb. We are then told about two or three lesser events occurring soon thereafter. Thenceforward there is nothing. For all the remainder of John's lifetime, we have no record whatever. There are some traditions, legends that may or may not hold elements of truth, but on the subject of John's life and labor, the scriptures are silent.

We do, however, have those New Testament books that bear John's byline, five of them, The Gospel, The Revelation, and three small epistles. What do these tell us about John's career? Nothing really. While these writings do not clarify the story of John's life, for some schools of scholarship, they actually complicate it. For the past century or more, there has been much debate, especially in regard to The Gospel and The Revelation.

Questions abound. Did John write the things credited to him, especially those two major ones? How could two writings so unalike have come from the same penman? Students and scholars have persistently wrestled with various aspects of these writings.

Why, for instance, is this gospel so different from the other three, the synoptics? So different is it, and the authorship so disputed, that it is often identified simply as The Fourth Gospel. Obviously, the author was a person of philosophic mind, superior command of language, and enormous writing skills. Did this younger son of Zebedee and Salome manage somehow to climb to such heights? If so, how?

The small book now in your hand will offer some answers for questions such as these. This book is about the apostle John, his life story. You may ask: With no historical record, how can we know the story? We cannot, of course; obviously, we can't. But there is much we do know.

We know much about John's early years, his character, and personal qualities. We know much about religious, cultural, and political conditions during his later years, and we know about forces and counterforces that played on directions and events. If we look carefully, we find numerous clues as to directions and events in the career of John. We will see him as a factor in a complicated world, in significant simultaneous relationship with three major national cultures, Hebrew, Greek, and Roman, with their divergent customs and laws.

This book will utilize what we know of this man, respect the traditions concerning him, consider all the circumstances of his time, and try to trace his career across the years. In this scenario all things come together easily, naturally; nothing is contrived, everything occurs sequentially, logically, and with cause.

But this is not history. With only a small part of it to be found in the ancient record, our scenario belongs in the category of historical fiction. Guided by all we know, we venture into the unknown, following always the pathways deemed most plausible, and sincerely asking: May there be other pathways more plausible than these?

The book will present this apostle as a man of true greatness, in full maturity, composed, educated, learned in philosophy, widely known, generally respected, and escaping martyrdom by reason of his integrity, intelligence, and towering level of manhood.

The book will find John to be the author of The Gospel and The Revelation, both written in response to real-life situations, and each a blockbuster in its time.

The book will discover why John's Gospel is so different from the other three and why The Revelation is so difficult for many to understand. Also it will show how John resolved an issue that had been for centuries a thorn in Greek philosophic thought, and how, with the same pen stroke, he answered that momentous question of Jesus: "Who do you say that I am?"

The book will see John, for much of his lifetime, as an active resident of Ephesus, with Athens, the world's premier intellectual center, only a short sea-sail away. And too, the book will see these writings of this apostle as the most significant source of encouragement and empowerment to come upon the Christian scene during those first difficult and hazardous years.

I

The harbor at Ephesus lay unrippled beneath the afternoon sun. At dockside two or three small ships lay lazily at anchor, and on the dock three tall young men stood silently gazing toward the open sea. Presently, the silence was broken by one who said, "Isn't that a sail l I see in the distance?"

There was excitement in the voice, and with equal excitement the others sprang to attention.

Indeed, there was a sail, and at length the ship itself appeared, a rather large vessel, drawing ever nearer, but slowly since that day there was little wind. Anxiously, the three young men glanced one to another. "Do you suppose...?" one said, and another replied, "I do hope so."

Eventually, the oncoming vessel was in the harbor; skilled seamen trimmed sail, and the ship glided silently to dockside. Even before she was fully at rest, one of the young men called to the ship's captain, "Do you come from Joppa, sir?"

The captain answered, "We do; shipped out three fortnights ago, put in only at Paphos and Patara."

Somewhat nervously, the voice came again from the dock, "Have you on board the apostle, sir?" and the captain replied, "We have."

On the dock, among the three, there was a flurry of exaltation and joy. One spoke to another, "Run quickly and bring word to the others."

By time of the disembarking, an assembly of twenty or more stood at the ship's side, awaiting the arrival of him whom the ship had brought. From the gunwale he saluted them. Then on the dock he stood among them, a man in age near fifty, a well-poised and gentle man, his beard and hair, once dark, now intermixed with gray.

Such was the arrival in Ephesus of the apostle John, and here on this day began a singular relationship that would endure for more than thirty years, and out of it would issue events of enormous consequence.

II

The apostle's arrival was an occasion fully worthy of the excitement it stirred. A dramatic moment, it was also a pivotal one. Much led up to it, and memorable happenings would later result from it. This is the story of these happenings; but first we must consider what came before. We must get to know John, the man, to view the circumstances that had brought him to the eminence on which he now stood.

Looking back, we see this young man, son of Zebedee and Salome, as a junior partner in a rather profitable fisheries business in Galilee, More than a fisherman, the young man was also an avid student, especially in the areas of Hebrew history and Greek language and culture. A frequent traveler to Jerusalem, he was ever striving for broader views and deeper insights.

When Jesus of Nazareth came calling, John was quick to answer that call. To John, it seemed that Jesus was pointing to something beyond, and being of adventurous and inquiring temper, he was quite willing to follow.

Actually, John and Jesus were first cousins. Jesus was a dozen years the older, and the two of them were, of course, not strangers to one another. So John became a disciple, a learner, this a natural pursuit for him, learner that by nature he was and would always be.

John followed Jesus very closely, enthusiastically in fact, and so impatiently that on one occasion Jesus called him and his brother "sons of thunder" and suggested they simmer down a bit. After three years of following, he had drawn very near, and then came that awful day at Mount Golgotha when John stood at the foot of a Roman cross and watched Jesus die. There were eleven or twelve apostles then, and John was the only one there.

The death of Jesus struck him hard and cut deeply. What he saw that day at Golgotha took the thunder all away and left in its place a sense of wonder and of awe that no circumstance could ever erase. The Golgotha experience was one he would never get over, nor would he ever try. Always a man to look beyond the obvious for deeper meanings, he tried hard, despite his anguish, to find such meanings now.

When the small band of disciples, mostly women, left that hilltop that day, it was on the arm of John that Mary, the mother of Jesus, was sustained. John was Mary's sister's son, and when dying Jesus had asked that, like a son, he assumed the care of Mary. In John's care Mary could feel secure, and together they could grieve their common loss; together they could ponder the meaning of it all, and this for many years they indeed would do.

John never felt Mary's care a burden, but always a privilege. Mary was a remarkable woman, astute, insightful; John was a young man of brilliant mind and sensitive spirit, and the two of them were as mother and son together.

Although both were Galileans, John welcomed Mary into his home in Jerusalem to reside for a good number of years. Mary never returned to Nazareth, her former home in Galilee. Joseph, Mary's faithful and ever-patient husband, previously married and much older than she, was now deceased, and his children, some of them at least, had never taken well to her. Actually, no older than some of them, she had been looked upon too much as an intruder in the family.

Mary's Nazareth neighbors, some of them especially, had never truly reconciled to the fact that Mary was pregnant with Jesus before she and Joseph were married. Perhaps they had not heard the unparalleled story of that pregnancy, or had they heard, they had not believed. When Jesus became well known as a teacher, some in and around Nazareth had become quite hostile, and these included many of Mary and Joseph's own family. For these and other reasons, Mary had little incentive to return to Nazareth.

She did, however, have several good reasons to remain in Jerusalem. A solitary member of the family, James, a devoted disciple, would remain there. Another James, John's older brother, Mary's nephew, would also remain in Jerusalem. There, too, were many disciples of Jesus, and a number of these, during recent days, had become Mary's personal friends. Uppermost, though, in Mary's mind was that here in Jerusalem were the scenes of her son's last momentous days.

Later, with the passing years, Mary's presence in Jerusalem would prove a significant blessing in that tentative and troubled community of Christian disciples, and very importantly, her encouragement and counsel would contribute largely to the making of the spiritual and intellectual giant that John would become.

As for John, his choice was Jerusalem also. Here his father, Zebedee, owned a house, and this would become home for him and his mother's sister. While he might continue to receive some income from the Galilean fisheries, John had known when he walked away from Mount Golgotha that Friday that his life and work would never be the same again. Three days later, with the astounding reappearance of Jesus, he was even more certain of it.

Although overwhelmed by all that had lately happened and perplexed by mysteries as yet unfathomed, one thing John knew and this he knew for sure: Henceforth the entire thrust of his life would be to sail on whatever ship his crucified cousin had just launched. And all things considered, John felt that the most suitable port from which to make his voyage was his country's center of religion and learning.

So here in Jerusalem, as time would tell, John would live, teach, and encourage the faith of those who had followed Jesus, often reviewing the story of him and also telling that story again and again to many who had never heard it. He therefore often traveled, and whether in Jerusalem or elsewhere, clusters of attentive listeners surrounded him and marveled at his word.

To tell the story of Jesus should have been for John a great joy, and in ways it was, but there were problems: There were those who did not wish that story told and were forever trying to silence those who told it. There were two groups of these. First, there were the powers that prevailed in Jerusalem, religious powers, who viewed the Christian movement as a threat to their long-held traditions and their deeply entrenched political and economic system. Second, there were the emperors who ruled the world from Rome, men who usually viewed themselves as divine and did not willingly tolerate other divinities.

Both of these powers would attempt, each in turn, to strangle the infant faith while it was yet in its cradle. After the suicide of Judas, ten of the eleven remaining apostles would be put to death; of the twelve, only John would survive to die naturally. He would first survive the persecutions that originated in Jerusalem. He would then, later, at Ephesus, encounter the hostile might of Rome, there to deal with imprisonments, banishments, and executions that were common in those years.

This youngest of the apostles, however, suffered his deepest pain during those earliest awful years. In AD 43, there in Jerusalem, under the brutal edict of Herod Agrippa I, John's brother James was put to death. The two brothers had been as close as brothers ever are. They had worked together in the Galilean fisheries business, and together they had walked three years with Jesus.

James had been the more volatile of the two, John the more quiet and introspective, and after the crucifixion and resurrection of Jesus, be had become more and more so. Then, too, his long association, like a son, with the mother of Jesus had strengthened his natural bent toward the philosophical. James had been the more visible and the more vocal; therefore, when the king wished to make an example of a disciple, it was James he chose. He imprisoned Simon Peter for a while, but it was James whose head was severed. John deeply felt the loss of his brother, and although untouched by Agrippa's purge, was quite aware of the danger in which he stood.

In the end, this quiet and gentle man, this poetic and thoughtful lover of the beautiful, would stand strong against the power of an empire and win over it a victory that would later encourage and inspire countless thousands.

III

As Jerusalem was the chief center of Hebrew religion and culture, the main hub of Greek culture and Roman influence in western Asia was Ephesus. Magnificent and important, Ephesus was the chief seaport on the Aegean coast. Primitive people had laid the foundations many centuries before, and more recently the Romans had come with their laws and customs.

Ephesus was now a part of the Roman Empire and the Romans were in complete control. Even before the Romans, though, the Greeks had come with their culture and their language, and as mighty as were the Romans, they had not been able to obliterate the Greek influence, nor had they really tried. Therefore, Ephesus now stood strong as a city of Greek culture and Roman law.

Ephesians were devoted to many gods, chief among these Artemis, whose monstrous temple towered in imposing splendor above everything else. While Roman emperors generally considered themselves divine, they apparently felt little threat from pagan shrines and temples; they were not much intimidated by marble statues. But when Christianity came along and began to grow in numbers and strength, they viewed this new religion with real alarm.

Here was a dynamic new faith with proven power to work drastic transformations in the attitudes, loyalties, and motivations of the people. Such power running loose in the empire was a very real threat; it could very quickly undercut an emperor's authority and break his hold over the population. As most emperors saw it, this was not to be allowed. Therefore, all who were devoted to the Christ were declared outlaws, to be dealt with severely.

Nevertheless, Christian communities multiplied rapidly throughout the empire, and Christian evangelists traveled widely both by land and sea. Most significant among these travelers was the intrepid disciple named Paul. His name was actually Saul, born at Tarsus 300 miles eastward from Ephesus, this dynamic activist was early a violent opponent of Christianity but later was transformed into a giant among witnesses for the faith he had once opposed.

Known as the apostle Paul, he was not actually an apostle but earned the title much as one who may be granted an honorary doctoral degree because he or she has achieved much.

In his travels, upon entering a community, Paul normally moved quickly to establish a vital cadre of the faithful and then move on. His travels eventually brought him to Ephesus, but this was neither a short stop nor a quick move. Here he remained and worked for more than two years, a great man powerfully touching the heart of a great city.

Although by ancestry a Jew, Paul was by birth a Roman. Having the advantages of Roman citizenship, he was able to move more freely and speak more openly than many of his fellow evangelists. Culturally savvy and highly educated, he fared well at Ephesus.

At length, however, answering a summons to new duties, Paul set sail from Ephesus and crossed the Aegean Sea to the cities of Macedonia and Greece. Ephesian Christians eagerly anticipated his early return. But this was not to be, either early or late; Paul would never again appear on the streets of Ephesus.

Instead, shortly after leaving there, it became apparent that the ever-circling enemies were closing around him; he clearly saw the end approaching. One compelling wish was to reach Jerusalem in time for that year's Passover festival, which he was certain would be his last.

Paul therefore turned eastward and recrossed the Aegean to the coast of Asia. Sailing southward along the shoreline, he would gladly have paused awhile with his friends at Ephesus but felt that rapidly moving events did not allow the visit. Instead, he made a brief stop at Miletus, thirty miles south. From that smaller seaport city, he sent messengers to Ephesus, asking that the leaders of that Christian community come to him there.

This they did, promptly and in large numbers, not then knowing what Paul had in mind to tell them. He would here give them the word they least wanted to hear; he would say goodbye. Worse, he would let them know that their teacher, spiritual father, and cherished friend was soon to face arrest, suffering, and possible death.

At Miletus that day Paul said, "I am on my way to Jerusalem, not knowing what will happen to me there, except that in every city imprisonments and persecutions are waiting for me. I know that none of you will ever see my face again."

Paul then offered some warnings and advice that his audience would never forget: "Keep watch over yourselves and all the flock. Savage wolves will come among you; therefore be alert."

When Paul had commended his friends to God's care, there was prayer and weeping. Then in deepest distress, the Ephesian disciples watched until the topmost sail of the apostle's ship disappeared into the southern sea.

It was a grief-stricken and troubled company who that day turned their faces northward and started home. Two powerful emotions engulfed them: grief for the loss of Paul and anxiety about their own future and the future of their faith.

This company of Ephesian Christians, like most of their fellows everywhere, lived under the pall of constant danger. They were a fledgling fellowship, standing precariously in the midst of powerful and hostile giants. Specifically, there were three of these.

First, there was Artemis, not her actually nor her statue or her temple, but the people who were devoted to her, some of them in particular. They viewed the Christian movement as a threat to them, as in ways it was. They had a passionate dislike for these Jesus-followers who insisted that Artemis was really not a god at all and was utterly unworthy of worship.

The Artemis people were especially irritated that a vibrant young religious community, having virtually no credentials, could entice many from the worship of Artemis to the discipleship of Christ. Of course, this exodus from their ranks had practical and financial consequences, and these they resented most. For example, during Paul's tenure at Ephesus, a silversmith named Demetrius had stirred a monumental ruckus because his small models of the goddess were not selling as well as previously. While hostile acts of the Artemis people were only occasional, this cult was nevertheless a constant concern for the Christians.

Of greater concern, however, was the more violent opposition of another religion: Judaism. Christianity, a child born of that faith, had not been generally accepted by the mother and was rejected actually. The ancient traditions could not yet accommodate the radically new and fundamentally different. Most of the earliest Christians were Jews, and their most vocal and sometimes most violent opponents, were those of their own family. Whether Gentile or Jew, the followers of Christ were everywhere put to great pain. Before his time in Ephesus, Paul had wrestled with these powers at places like Antioch Psidia, Iconium, Lystra, and Philippi.

Now, though, as the Ephesian leaders took their troubled way from Miletus to Ephesus, another and even greater power loomed over them. The infamous Nero was emperor of Rome, and the Roman resolve to obliterate Christianity had reached a new level of intensity.

Sometimes, for their own reasons, the Romans brought charges against the Christians and inflicted the punishments, and on other occasions they willingly imposed penalties on charges brought by the Jewish authorities. Roman and Jewish authorities had little in common, but in regard to the Christian issue they were usually in agreement. Each, for their own reasons, saw Christianity as a threat to be dealt with harshly and decisively.

It was therefore a somber occasion when the Ephesian elders, having bidden farewell to Paul at Miletus, arrived at home and reported to their comrades there: Paul would not return, not ever again.

Hostile forces surrounded them; they felt they were newly orphaned in a strange and dangerous world. Without the confident leadership of Paul, how could they cope with all the towering giants that surrounded them?

IV

Only days afterward, as the whole assembly was gathered, one of the company offered a striking suggestion. It received unanimous attention instantly. Might it be possible that the apostle John could come and help them for a while? He had been at several cities in Asia Minor, but never at Ephesus. Some of the group had heard him speak, a few had met him, and most had read some of the messages he had written. They knew that his home was in Jerusalem and that he sometimes traveled. If only he might come to them! It was quickly agreed: They would ask him.

A few weeks afterward, five of the Ephesian elders were in Jerusalem speaking with John: Would he please consider coming to Ephesus? Almost immediately John sensed the invitation as providential. Reasons for his remaining in Jerusalem had largely evaporated over time.

Only a short while before, Mary, the beloved Mother of Jesus, had gracefully surrendered to the assault of age and illness, and her death had been deeply felt by John. Also, Jerusalem was now seething with the discontent and intrigue that would, six years later, result in a full-scale Jewish revolt against Rome, and this in turn would result, four years after that, in the virtual destruction of Jerusalem by Emperor Vespatian's Roman legions.

Many residents, among these many disciples, had already fled the city, as would many more a little later. However, James, a member of Mary's own family, would remain in Jerusalem. Among the disciples, he had risen to a position of trust and leadership, and it was of much comfort to John that he would be available to the disciples remaining there.

So, would John respond to the Ephesian call? Yes, he would. But first he would bid farewell to many disciples in areas around Jerusalem, Antioch, and Caeserea. Only a short while before, the apostle Paul had arrived in the city, soon to face arrest and to be involved in legal proceedings that would continue for more than two years. From here he would later be taken to Rome, a prisoner. From here, too, John would soon travel to Ephesus for many years of life and labor.

For this brief interlude, however, both men would be in or near Jerusalem, and often together. Paul would grieve that, unlike John, he had never seen Jesus or heard his voice, and would seek from John all he knew of their Lord. John, with equal eagerness, would probe Paul's memory of his evangelistic tours of many lands. The men would rejoice together in the transforming power they had found in their Christ and would deeply feel their burden of responsibility to make that power known. At length, they would be confident in parting that they would never meet again.

John's final pause before leaving Judea would be at the home of Philip in Caeserea. Here the community of disciples would gather and bid him affectionate farewell, and from here he would travel down the coast to Joppa and the ship that would carry him away to Ephesus.

Now, therefore, receiving from John the answer they had hoped, the Ephesian elders could go home to await his coming. This they did; and in Ephesus all the disciples joined in the waiting, eagerly anticipating.

And so it was that about three months later, three young men stood on the Ephesian dock searching the horizon, and there detected tall sails in the distance. And as the ship glided to dockside, they shouted their question, "Have you on board the apostle, sir?" and heard the captain's reply, "We have."

V

Before the passing of many days, anxious elders approached the apostle with an urgent question: "How long can you be with us, Brother John?"

Asking their question, these men were not altogether sure they wanted to hear John's reply. But when his answer came, as it promptly did, they were borne up on a surging tide of joy. John said, "With your generosity and God's grace, I shall make your community my home until the Spirit may sometime call me away."

So the apostle John became a resident of Ephesus. Here he would assume leadership of the Christian community, this not by appointment or election but by the natural consequence of his being who he was, not merely as one who had walked with Jesus but chiefly for his rare qualities of character and demeanor. Quietly, thoughtfully, in the gentle manner that was his, he went about among his fellow disciples, always offering comfort and encouragement.

The tendency among them was to accord him a certain deference, even a reverence. Rejecting this, he would often ask, "Who am I?" and then answer, "I am simply a disciple whom Jesus loved." Then he would add, "So are you — so are we all."

Thus it came about within the community of Ephesian disciples that this spiritual and intellectual giant was soon known to most simply as "Brother John." There would, however, always be a certain awe in the way the people pronounced those words. There would ever be the inescapable awareness that a singular human being moved and worked among them.

In the city, on the streets, and in the public places, the apostle was soon known to most informed citizens. Most, however, did not think of him as the premier Christian in the area but rather as a philosopher or as a quiet fatherly type of man of philosophical temper. The Greek influence was such that the philosophical was respectfully regarded, and John's manner of gospel presentation was usually well accepted.

When Athenian thinkers crossed the Aegean to visit Ephesus, they usually inquired for John and spent time with him. During his many years at Ephesus, John himself sometimes made the short voyage across the sea to Athens for visits at the Aeropagua. The apostle Paul had earlier experienced a rather cordial welcome there, and now likewise John on various occasions. While Roman authorities were usually hostile, Jewish traditionalists unyieldingly critical, and the Artemis people somewhere between indifferent and violent, the Athenian heirs of Plato were openly seekers for truth and were quite willing, eager really, to consider any new thing.

John often quoted Jesus as saying, "I am the truth." The Athenians found this profoundly fascinating, and most of them respected John as a fellow philosopher. In whatever company, philosophical or otherwise, there was never any question, though, as to the deep convictions that possessed the man. John was utterly certain that grace and truth had been manifest in Jesus Christ and that indeed it would be he who would somehow transform and purify the world.

Others, saying these things, usually encountered hostility, but not John, not often anyway. People heard him respectfully, not always believingly, but almost never resentfully. They who heard him did not always understand, but they were normally convinced that he understood. Never glib of speech, John always appeared to speak from having thought, and one who heard him was likely to say, "If I can think deeply as this man thinks, perhaps I too can understand." There were, however, many who did understand and to whom the message of John came like a new light dawning.

It seemed that John always pitched the Christian message an octave or two deeper than most. Done in his gentle, loving, confident, grandfatherly way, most conversationalists found it difficult to argue with him and even more difficult to be angry with him.

As the apostle Paul had sometimes been somewhat sheltered from attack by his Roman citizenship, John was now to some extent protected by his rare personal qualities, so compelling as to silence most hostile voices. Thus, John would enjoy many years as virtually the sage of Ephesus.

VI

While during those many years at Ephesus John made numerous voyages across the Aegean to Greece, these were not the most significant of his travels. More importantly, he often traveled overland to visit various Christian communities in Asia Minor. There were within less than ninety miles of Ephesus at least half a dozen cities where the forward-marching faith had established firm footholds.

At these points, close-knit groups of disciples struggled to comprehend the deep meanings of their faith and to deal with powerful forces that opposed it. All these needed such guidance and support as the great apostle might give them. Generously responding to such needs, John traveled a wide circuit.

As his communion with the philosophical sharpened John's thought and confirmed his commitment, his labors among his people became the wellspring from which his greatest achievements would later flow. Within the Christian communities, where peace and calm should always have prevailed, there were sometimes storms. For John, dealing with the storms proved the better builder of the strengths that would serve him so well later.

There was, for instance, the city of Thyatira. Here, not more than 75 miles from Ephesus, the prevailing deity was not Artemis but her twin brother Apollo. Apollo had always had trouble with human females and they with him. Everyone understood that Daphane, Coronis, Cassandra, and others had fatefully run afoul of his wanton ways. In the real life of real people, his female devotees were sometimes disastrously affected by the character of their god.

At Thyatira, one of these had come into the Christian fellowship and had brought with her some dark character flaws. In the church, attracting a company of cronies who passionately followed her, she had effectively split the Thyatiran fellowship into two contending parties.

To most of the people, so obnoxious was this woman that they hesitated even to pronounce her name; in horror of her despicable character, they derisively spoke of her, when they spoke of her at all, simply as "that woman." Later, John would give her a name, choosing the most distasteful one any Israelite had ever known, *Jezebel*. "That woman *Jezebel*," he would say.

Struggle with it as he would and did, the problem of *Jezebel* was one John was never able to solve. To be sure, some of her brainwashed and debauched followers were indeed reclaimed for the Christ, but many never were. Such was the sort of heartache that would lie like a stone for many years upon the spirit of the apostle. Most people, however, who knew or observed the man would never have known of this and other burdens that he bore.

There was, too, the multi-faceted situation at another of the cities. Here there were two groups of error mongers, both trying to undercut the foundations of the faith and each at loggerheads with the other. One of these groups was the Baalamites, an occult type who claimed superior knowledge of everything. People who profess exclusive direct access to some private source of insight are rather hard to reach with any truth, and with the Baalamites John found it so.

At Laodecea, however, there was heartbreak of another kind. Antipas was a rather prominent Roman who had dramatically converted to Christianity, quickly becoming a powerful witness for Christ. Other Romans may have felt betrayed — surely they were resentful; regardless, they turned on their fellow Roman and killed him. John would later speak of him as a "faithful martyr."

Others of the faithful in the Laodecean community found it difficult to deal with the martyrdom of Antipas. Among them there was a mingling of grief, sorrow, anger, bewilderment, and especially a profound anxiety: What hostile acts would next occur?

Christian discipleship being what it was, it seemed to John that every community of disciples should be a haven of peace. But it was not always so, and the loving, trustful apostle found every sinew of his being wrenched by this brutal fact. How could some people be of such mean spirit? John's was a feeling of compassion for them, a sorrow, a deep sadness; they were missing so much that was so good. It was a mystery to John; it was so contrary to all he was and all he felt; he could never understand it and was to the end perplexed and troubled by it. Nevertheless, with passing time, the serene and gentle apostle became only more and more so.

VII

The world of John's time, however, was not an easy world to be serene and gentle in. That world was, of course, ruled from Rome, and during the fourteen years from 54 to 68 Nero was the emperor there. Apparently without conscience, the man freely practiced every form of infamy. In the empire he ruled, no person could ever feel safe or secure, and Christian disciples especially stood in constant peril. It had been, in fact, during the early part of Nero's reign that the ever-circling enemies began to close around Paul.

Now, early in John's tenure at Ephesus, actually in the year 64, came the news that an enormous fire had destroyed much of Rome, the city, and that Nero had declared the Christians responsible for it. Paul had barely arrived in the city — as a prisoner — and uppermost in every Christian mind was the question: What would now befall him there?

Two years later, in the year 66, the Jewish people of Judea launched all-out rebellion against Nero's Roman rule, and for half a dozen years the land was ravaged by total war. The disciples at Ephesus, especially the Jewish among them, were deeply troubled by the horrible news brought by every incoming ship. Two powerful emotions surged within them. First was the pain they suffered for the ruin of their homeland and their people, their family. Second, there was the agonizing question: What penalties would the Romans next vindictively impose upon Jewish people everywhere? After all, Christians, most of whom were Jewish, were under condemnation already, and would all Judaism now fall before that same judgment? Given the character of the psychopath who ruled in Rome, no one could guess what edict may next be issued. Over the Ephesian disciples, as over all disciples everywhere, hung a heavy cloud of uncertainty and anxiety.

Still, though, a heavier blow was about to fall and soon did. Only months after the onset of the war in Judea came word from Rome that Paul was dead, beheaded by order of Nero. As always, seeing beyond the obvious, John spoke quietly: "Yes, our brother Paul is dead; but our Lord lives; and as for us, we too shall die; and because he lives, so shall we, and now beyond death so does our brother Paul."

Some found comfort in John's word; most were somewhat reassured by his calm demeanor; yet almost everyone felt the smothering oppressiveness of awesome powers that seemed to be always in control and always victorious.

This ominous foreboding became almost overwhelming only a little later with news that Simon Peter, like Paul, was also dead, also cut down by Roman might. Like Paul, Peter had been in Rome, not as a prisoner but as an evangelist working somewhat secretly among the people.

Already deeply distressed and to some extent discouraged by the sufferings imposed upon disciples everywhere, Peter had found the execution of Paul momentarily plunging him into a dark pit of despair. Remembering, though, the sufferings and crucifixion of Jesus, he had soon recovered his courage and had heroically died on a Roman cross.

Ah! the power of Rome, the brutal force falling first here, then there, and apparently at length everywhere. To the Ephesian disciples, it appeared the Romans were invincible, their word final, against their judgments no appeal. It was commonly known that Rome deemed herself eternal, and to almost everyone throughout the world, especially Christians, it seemed that indeed she was.

That feeling was relieved a little when, only months after Peter's death, Nero took his own life. The next ruler of note was Vespasian, not a bad one really; nevertheless, the war in Judea raged on, and the ancient mountains and village streets were still red with the many spillings of Jewish blood. Messengers often brought tidings of friends and kindred who had died in that struggle for freedom.

Ill as the news of war was, the worst came in Vespasian's second year: Jerusalem had fallen. And worse yet, the temple had been destroyed. For a thousand years, their seemingly eternal symbol of home and hope, sometimes devastated but always rebuilt, the temple had now gone down, and it was the conviction of almost all the Ephesians that it would never rise again.

Deeply, the Jewish Christians of Ephesus grieved their losses; but why was this grief so deep? After all, it had been Jerusalem and fellow-Jews who had stoned Stephen and beheaded James and for thirty years had laid harsh punishments upon disciples everywhere. Yes, they had indeed been hostile and in many ways had cast themselves in the role of enemy; but nevertheless, there was this overarching fact: They were family.

They were, all of them, like these of Ephesus, the children of father Israel. Besides, it had been only those in positions of authority, not the common people, who had been so hostile. Now, for these in Ephesus, it was painful to know that those in Judea were forced from their homes and their country, to find refuge wherever in the world they could.

The conviction was firm among Ephesian disciples that the sufferings inflicted upon them by their fellow-Jews were now a hundredfold eclipsed by the sufferings Rome was inflicting not only upon Christians but upon Jews as well. It seemed to them that Rome was not content merely to strangle the infant in its cradle but must also slay the mother.

Among the thousands now fleeing Judea, there were many who made their way to Ephesus. Some of these were disciples and some were not, but all were welcomed into the Christian community there. Most who were not disciples when they came soon were, and so did the dispersion add momentum to the growing and ever-spreading fellowship of disciples everywhere.

In Judea, however, there were those who would neither surrender to the Romans nor flee their land. About a thousand of these took refuge in an old fortress atop Mount Masada. After an assault lasting months, the Romans at last scaled the cliffs, and rather than surrender, these thousand took their own lives.

As these breathed their last, the final breath went also out of all Jewish resistance. Rome had won, Rome the all-powerful, Rome the forever invincible, or so it seemed.

It appeared that the followers of Jesus would be forever a struggling group of the hounded and hunted, and their vision of righteousness, peace, and a glorious kingdom forever only a dream, with no hope that a brighter day could ever dawn. The awesome power of the Romans and all the Roman-like was simply too great, or so it seemed.

John's prayer, often heard by those around him, was this: "O Lord, we see the storm; we feel the dark and the danger; but give us, we pray, eyes to see beyond." He would then speak to the people, and over and over again he would say, "The end is not yet; power will not win; love will. Therefore, children, love one another, and in love reach out to all."

Great as was the difficulty of being serene and gentle under the rule of first-century Rome, the apostle John continued to be so. The Ephesian years were one long, unrelenting tension between harsh realities apparent on every side and the faith that could foresee their ending. John held fast that faith, but it was difficult to convince others of it.

For many, faith was no match for the monster that was Rome, surely a monster in size and power, and in the mind of most Christians, also a monster in evil doings. Despite the assurances and comforts of faith, the dark specter of apprehension and anxiety overhung everything. Truly, not even the best informed could ever know what a day would bring forth. In the minds of many men much of the time seethed a haunting question: Since yesterday they took my neighbor away for imprisonment, exile, or death, will they come for me tomorrow?

VIII

In this precarious circumstance, the Ephesian disciples made their uncertain way from day to day, and under this dark pall of foreboding the apostle John quietly and calmly went about his work.

One day John would offer the comforts of faith to a woman whose husband had just been taken away for a fate as yet unknown, and the next he would perhaps embrace a newly orphaned child. Sometimes he sat with families, pleading with them the cause of faith against the stark realities of Roman might. Daily he met with confused and fearful groups who often sought his guidance for surviving in a dark time while waiting for a light it seemed would never dawn.

Sometimes John stood as mediator between the Jewish who were disciples and the Jewish who were not. Instigated by the hierarchy centered in Jerusalem, some leaders in various localities had participated in the persecution of disciples, Gentile and Jewish alike. However, with the Roman victory of the year 70, such organized persecution virtually ceased, leaving only enclaves of the hostile here and there.

There were at Ephesus Jews of the ancient tradition and Jews of the new Faith, and mostly the two groups lived together as neighbors, as family and friends. On occasion, however, troublesome issues flared, and John's voice was usually a calming force in such storms. As a result of the apostle's closely reasoned and gentle treatment of the problems, not only were hostilities often healed, but also, amid much rejoicing, many of the formerly hostile embraced the Faith they had once so much resented.

It was never necessary for John to persuade his people to "go to church." They gathered willingly, even eagerly, and as frequently as possible. All of them in constant danger, the people urgently needed one another; there was so much against them that they passionately desired that nothing come between them. From one another, in true communion, they drew strength and in their gatherings found comfort. There were occasional exceptions, of course, and these troubled John greatly.

The Jesus people of Ephesus well knew that their assemblies were a defiance of Roman law, and they knew also the awful punishments that could be levied against them. Yet they assembled; so important to them and so precious was their gathering together that they risked their very lives for the privilege. Nor did John seek to spare them; he never discouraged their assembling; he was in a danger as great or greater than any of them, and he knew this and so did they. First of all they were a fellowship, and best of all John was with them.

The Artemis people had their temple and the people of Judaism their synagogues, but for their gatherings the Jesus people had only their homes and a few private places. Earlier the disciples, especially the Jewish among them, had continued their life-long custom of synagogue worship on the week's seventh day. As they became less and less welcome in the synagogues, they also became less and less satisfied with that ancient ritual.

Feeling the need for something more, they also gathered more privately on the week's first day. And why the first day rather than some other? Because it was on this day that Jesus had come alive after death. For these Ephesian disciples, as for all everywhere, that resurrection was of paramount importance. This was their Faith's first fact, always an event to celebrate, and celebrate they did, weekly. And so doing they established a practice that has survived for two millennia.

This first-day assembly was strongly encouraged by John, and week after week the people heard John speak of that first day some thirty years before. Again and again, conveyed in one phrase or another, they heard John's calm and considered word: "Had the life of Jesus ended with his death, we who followed would have returned to our fishing, grieving our loss, with only sadness in our hearts and no song on our lips. But, having died, instead of going away as the dead have always done, he came back, he came back to us, and we saw him and we knew him."

"And please understand this," John would say. "Having overcome death, he has also overcome all enemies this side of that. Thus, as we celebrate his victory, we also celebrate our own. And incidentally, although Caesar does not know it yet, mighty Rome has been defeated already." John's people tried hard to believe him but found it terribly difficult.

IX

There was during John's Ephesus years an explosion of literary activity among Christian leaders. Earlier Paul had written extensively and several others somewhat, mostly occasional communications of practical nature. Now, following the executions of Paul and Peter, literary effort quite suddenly turned historical, with a specific focus on the life, activities, and actual teachings of Jesus.

Soon after the crucifixion of Simon Peter, a large papyrus scroll was received in Ephesus, coming from Rome. The lettering was impeccable Greek, and whether an original document or a copy was neither certain or really important to the Ephesian disciples.

The document itself, though, whether original or not, was of highest importance to all the Ephesians, and especially so to the apostle John. He instantly recognized the circumstances under which the writing had been done, the purpose of it, and the great significance.

Commonly, Christian writings were copied and recopied, then circulated among disciples everywhere, and John had seen many of these. This one, however, he instantly identified as of singular importance. Not far into the manuscript he came upon a passage concerning himself, reference to an episode of many years before. He read: "Jesus came to Galilee... and he walked beside the sea, and he saw Simon and Andrew his brother casting a net... and he said to them, 'Follow me,' and immediately they left their nets and followed him. As he went a little farther, he saw James the son of Zebedee and his brother John.... Immediately he called them, and they left their father... and followed him."

Reading this, John sat a long while, remembering. Speaking to himself, he said, "Yes, so it was, so it is; I left and I followed." After a long, thoughtful pause, he whispered, "And now I follow on." Then for a little while his eyes were too moist for reading.

The document John had before him then we now know as the gospel according to Saint Mark. The youthful John Mark had been an early follower of Jesus but had been somewhat ambivalent about it. After a bit of floundering, though, he soon found his way, drew up close to him he followed, and remained there for the balance of his life. Associated with three or four of the apostles and learning much from them, he had at last become the younger apprentice of Simon Peter. He had listened attentively to all Peter had said about Jesus and had made copious notes concerning what he heard.

John Mark had long known that his mentor and teacher had desired to write what he knew of Jesus' life but had always hesitated, feeling himself unworthy, and at last had been executed before undertaking the task. Now, in great degree as tribute to Simon Peter, John Mark had written what he had long hoped the apostle would.

The apostle John was deeply saddened that Peter's voice was now forever stilled but thankful for the testimony of his young protégé. Nevertheless, John longed for the day when actually someone of the twelve would tell the story all of them had lived, felt, and suffered through — to that one ultimate victory at the last.

Not long after the appearance of Mark's work, there appeared a second account of the life of Jesus. This one, like

Mark's, was not written by an apostle. As Mark had been closely associated with Peter, Luke had been closely related to Paul, his assistant, traveling companion, and personal physician; and now disciples everywhere were reading his version of the story.

Luke's manuscript coming into the hands of John, he read: "Since many have undertaken to set down an orderly account of the events that have been fulfilled among us, just as they were handed on to us by those who at the beginning were eyewitnesses and servants of the word, I too decided, after investigating everything carefully from the very first, to write an orderly account."

Having read this, John then read it a second time and then a third. He then put the manuscript aside and considered it for a long time: No, like Mark, Luke had not been an eyewitness; for that matter, neither had Paul; they had missed so much; now "after investigating everything carefully," Luke would write; How like a physician, John thought: first diagnosis, then action; and with that thought John smiled and read on.

Like the record of Mark, Luke's was credible; but neither writer, John felt, had mined the subject to its depths. Both had commendably reported many episodes from the life of Jesus; but who was he really? John was pleased with what he read but felt deeply that more should be said. After all, Luke had never known the Jesus he had known so well.

The apostle Matthew was now 29 years deceased, martyred. Over in Syria, even his youngest protégés were growing old. Fondly remembering all their revered teacher had told them, these felt that they should write as they were convinced Matthew would have written. This they did, and like Matthew, being deeply imbued with the traditions of Judaism, they set Jesus in historical context, declaring him Israel's long-anticipated Messiah.

Reading what they wrote, John was deeply thankful for the truth of it but also somewhat distressed. It was good, indeed, to declare Jesus the culmination of a notable past; but what of the future? Who was Jesus in relation to that? In the deep places of his mind, John had long pondered the question: Who is Jesus really, and what is the meaning of him? And from equally deep, the answer had come: I know that I know; but by what power of language can such truth be told?

Many years before, when the apostles were walking one day with Jesus on the road to Jerusalem, John and his brother had ventured to request a cousinly favor of their cousin Jesus, and to their request Jesus had replied: "You do not know what you ask." From that day onward, John had never been a man to put himself forward.

For those many years John had been content to follow, was never inclined to push his way to the front of anything. Now he wrestled with a vexing question: Should he undertake to write what he knew and understood of Jesus?

Of this John was absolutely certain: Any account of Jesus he would write could never be a common variety of biography; he could never be satisfied merely to recite episodes from that life; he would necessarily write in such a way that any reader would know Jesus, truly know him; he would probe deeply for truth, and he would have to be philosophical about it.

To great length and in great depth, John pondered the matter. Would he undertake the task? After long hesitation, at last the answer came: Yes, he would.

X

Lifelong, the apostle John always had eyes for seeing beyond the obvious. During his three years with Jesus and the others, he had, of course, witnessed many of the things Jesus did and said. In all of this, he characteristically saw more than most others saw. Earlier than most, he was convinced that Jesus was more than another rabbi in a long line of rabbis, that he was somewhat more than a crusader against Roman tyranny, and that he was, in fact, somewhat more than he himself and all the other apostles and all other men. That Friday at Mount Golgotha he had been more deeply convinced, and three days afterward absolutely sure.

Once Jesus had questioned his disciples, saying, "Who do you say that I am?" There had been scarcely a day during all the intervening years in which John had not relived that moment and reconsidered that question, and he knew now that he could never write the story of Jesus without offering an answer to it.

John was sure he knew the answer; he had no doubt of that. But the answer being what it was, never before in all history had language been called upon to express what John must now undertake to say.

He knew several languages well, and was especially fluent in three: Hebrew, Aramaic, and Greek. Of all languages, Greek was the most refined, most precise, and for 500 years had been the world's premier vehicle for artistic and philosophical expression. In John's day, Greek was a kind of universal language; whatever other language they may have spoken, all educated and cultivated people also spoke Greek, and if it may be said that thinking people think in a language, it was in Greek that they thought.

Nor did they avoid difficult subjects. Among other awesome topics, they probed and pondered the origin, character, and destiny of being, be-ing, existence, is-ness. Six hundred years before John, the Greek philosopher Heraclitus had concluded that no material being could be thought of apart from an "other." He had taught that implicit in the cosmos was a "divine reason" ordering it and giving it form and meaning. He had discerned in the cosmic process a factor not unlike the reasoning power of the human mind.

This Heraclitus named the *logos*. Without *logos* nothing could be. But what was it?

For more than half a millennium, subsequent thinkers had wrestled with the questions Heraclitus had raised, and invariably they pondered the mystery of being. Doing so, they came again and again to that tantalizing Greek concept, that tantalizing Greek word *logos*. Over and over, they attempted to probe the depths, but never could go deeper than the mystery that lay somewhere in the depths of that word itself.

The quest was fully apparent in the tide of Greek philosophy that rose to its pinnacle with Plato and Aristotle. A little later, it figured largely in the thinking of Zeno and Epicurus and various others.

The earliest attempts at defining words were primitive dictionaries developed by the Greeks at about John's time. Then, as later, *logos* was defined as *reason*, or *word*, or *mind*. All such definitions, though, were universally recognized as inadequate. In those intellectual struggles, *logos* was always unavoidable, inescapable, but always remained a mystery.

There had been no agreement on one basic question: Was *logos* material or immaterial? As John had increasingly given his magnificent mind to philosophical studies, he had much earlier reached a firm conclusion: *logos* was personal.

Now, as the apostle would attempt to write of Jesus, he would say who he believed Jesus to be, to answer the awful question Jesus had asked of his followers: Who do you say that I am? Hearing this, Simon Peter had answered, "You are the Messiah," meaning of course, "the Christ, the anointed one." But who indeed was this one, this one anointed? This deeper question was the one John felt he must answer.

His answer, he believed, would also answer the question raised by Heraclitus and long debated by others. He would put forward his answer as clearly and forcefully as possible, nor would he delay until the end of the story; he would begin with it. And after years of thought and unrelenting study, he was confident that he had at last the language for the task. He was not sure his answer would ever be understood; but he had to try.

Inevitably almost, as the apostle John applied pen to papyrus, the very first words he wrote in Greek characters were these: "In the beginning was the *logos*."

Virtually all the philosophers of the previous centuries would have been pleased with John's opening phrase. Then John went on: "And the *Logos* was with God, and the *Logos was* God." They would have been fascinated with that but would have been of uncertain opinion about it. Next came John's word: "All things came into being through him." Mostly, the thinkers would have been intrigued by his view of the beginning of being but would have been startled by John's use of the personal pronoun *him*, not the *it* of most earlier discussions.

Their greater shock, however, would have occurred a few sentences later when they read, "The *Logos* became flesh and dwelt among us." Here was John's blockbuster. The *logos* personal and present? This was new: philosophers had never even dreamed it. But here was the apostle saying: Here it is, a new truth; the ageless *Logos* has stepped into time, and he is with us.

John had said it concisely and clearly: "The *Logos* became flesh and dwelt among us." With that short sentence, John had also given his answer to the unanswered question of Jesus: "Who do you say that I am?"

Other Christian writers had told something of the birth of Jesus, but John would say nothing of this; for him the manner of the birth was a mere incidental. John was not much concerned with stories of shepherds and magi, but with what really happened that night at Bethlehem. For him, singing angels and a shining star were but outward flags, mere signs of the real event.

What was really happening there? John was absolutely sure of it and would say so: **God was so loving the world that he was giving his own.** More than this, saying it with even greater force, **the *Logos* was becoming flesh.**

Thus, the apostle John, youngest and brightest of the disciples of Jesus, would call upon the most profound concept of Greek philosophy to proclaim the grandest truth of Christian faith. More than this, he would, virtually in a single pen stroke, answer philosophy's oldest and most salient question and Christendom's newest and most pressing one.

The apostle would face head-on the two most perplexing questions of his time. On the one hand, disciples of Jesus were asking: Who is Jesus, really? And John answered: He is the *Logos*. On the other hand, philosophers, even from ancient time, were still asking: What is the *Logos*, really? And John's answer very explicitly addressed their question: The *Logos* is the Christ, who from the beginning was with God and was God, and without whom nothing was made that was made. So did this remarkable man examine both questions and find that each answered the other.

XI

The apostle's profound interpretation of Jesus burst explosively upon both the religious and philosophical worlds. It received immediate attention on both sides of the Aegean Sea, stirring deep thought among Christians and philosophers alike. In Rome and among Roman officials, however, it stirred little thought, for as among most power brokers, these were not exactly famous as great thinkers. They were, though, even worried, scared.

Twenty-seven years had passed since Nero's suicide and 26 since the brutal Galba's murder. For ten years, the Roman empire had been ruled, quite responsibly, by Vespasion, who had been succeeded by his son Titus. After less than two years, though, Titus had been assassinated by Domitian, his own brother, who assumed the throne and would rule with ever-increasing perfidy for fifteen terrible years, until his own murder in the year 96.

It was in Domitian's final year that John's blockbuster book came to the attention of authorities in Rome. Roman officials both in the capital city and in Ephesus had long known of John and had looked upon him as a gentle, likable, elderly philosopher who moved somewhat harmlessly about in philosophical and religious circles. They suddenly realized that they had not really known the man; suddenly they saw him in a different light.

While already widely known and highly respected, John was now almost instantly famous, or as the Roman authorities viewed him, infamous. This one-time fisherman at a small Galilean lake had emerged from a background of quiet pastoral labor into the limelight, a major champion and hero of an outlawed religious faith. As the Romans saw it, John's growing sphere of influence was a threat too great. They most feared his likely appeal to the learned and the elite of the empire. Their final word was this: The apostle was to be no longer tolerated.

The message was not long coming. The proconsul of Asia, at his headquarters in Ephesus, soon received the word from Rome: Give immediate attention to the problem of the aged apostle. Immediate attention, though, was not forthcoming; the proconsul hesitated; John was loved and trusted by many people; there could be a troublesome outcry.

That cry could come from voices other than the Christian. Many Roman citizens in the provinces, especially in Achaia and Asia, deeply resented the Roman policy in regard to the Christians who lived among them. Those selected for punishment were often good neighbors, good friends, and sometimes relatives. Earlier, in some areas, disciples had attempted to live together in enclaves, but that era now past, they were homemakers, gardeners, tanners, tent-makers, shopkeepers, and active participants in their communities. Most disciples were not looked upon by their neighbors as they were seen from Rome.

Although the proconsul was fearful of possible disturbances, he was first of all a servant of the empire, and risk of local tumult was a risk he was often compelled to take. Therefore, not long after the order came, he sent his centurion and a contingent of ten for the arresting of John. A solitary soldier could have done it just as well.

John had carefully prepared his people for this hour. For many weeks, John and the Ephesian disciples, correctly reading the signs, had assumed that soldiers would one day come. John had calmly, as usual, gone about among his people comforting and encouraging them. When they had expressed dismay about the awful peril in which John now stood, his response was to say, "You know that neither Paul nor I nor any man can be with you forever, but you do know, do you not, that our Lord will be with you always."

When the disciples had pressed John for his own feeling about what lay ahead for him, he simply said, "For whatever reason, I cannot suffer more than Jesus suffered for us all." John had tried diligently to teach his people to see beyond the immediate circumstance, however dreadful, and to anticipate the joy that always lay somewhere beyond the pain.

Thus, when the soldiers came for John, reconciliations had already been mostly made. To his arrest John offered no more resistance than Jesus had offered to his. As for John's people, they stood by and looked once again upon his face, calm, serene. But there were tears here and there among them. Thirty years before, these people, at Miletus, had said tearful farewell to one revered apostle, Paul, and now at Ephesus, they would bid tearful farewell to another, John.

What punishment would the Romans now impose upon him? Perhaps an enormous fine that would take from him all things that he possessed, as affecting John a very small punishment indeed, for he possessed little; perhaps they would imprison him somewhere; or perhaps, as they sometimes did, they would pronounce the death sentence, as they had upon both Paul and Peter. As the soldiers took John away, neither he nor any of the disciples knew to what destination they were going.

At dockside in the Ephesus harbor stood a huge dark ship with the Roman ensign at its prow. To this ship John was taken and with other prisoners held in the dark below the decks. Some, like him, were disciples, and others were thieves or seditionists or murderers who had violated one or more of the Roman laws or were believed by the Romans to have done so.

Sails unfurled, the ship moved slowly away, and off shore in the open sea it turned south toward Patmos. Patmos was an island 37 miles southwest of Miletus, a six-by-ten-mile mass of rocky volcanic hills. The island was a Roman prison whose walls on every side were many miles of open sea. Here a small garrison of Romans could maintain control of hundreds of Rome's real and imagined enemies. Here the Roman ship would dock, and here, presumably, the apostle John would waste away his few remaining years.

However, it would not be so. For this was John, the apostle John, whose spirit would soar above the highest peaks of Patmos, whose vision would reach far beyond the surrounding sea.

XII

On Patmos, for the general prison population, there were no cells and no bars. On occasion, however, men who had become violent or who had fallen into disfavor with the guards were seized and restrained, often cruelly. Near the southern extremity of the island stood a cluster of long, low structures of dark volcanic stone where these were held, and here also soldiers were quartered and administrative offices maintained.

Almost all prisoners were free to wander about. They were required only to gather for bed checks at night. In groups of no more than five, conversations among inmates were permitted. John soon found that most prisoners appeared to be rather normal types of men, that many, like himself, were held here for no crime other than being disciples of Jesus.

For these, though, there was a special restriction: They were not permitted to promote their faith in any way or even discuss it among themselves or with others. For these who so urgently needed the fellowship of one another, this prohibition was equally as burdensome as prison itself.

Many disciples, though, found subtle ways of communicating with others, John among them. Within days of his arrival, John was going about offering quiet words of encouragement everywhere, even in quaint and clever ways to the guards themselves.

John's was a commanding presence among disciples and among others as well. All who met him took notice: the simple gesture of an open hand, the polite nod to one in passing, the slow smile that sometimes lightly touched his lips, eyes that were often lit as with a light from somewhere beyond, the aura of a latent something that seemed to lie deep within the man.

Thus, within his first week on Patmos, the apostle became generally known. Although most did not know his name, his fellow prisoners understood that a remarkable man moved among them. Concerning his identity, however, the Roman authorities were fully informed, or believed they were. They knew him, or thought they did, as an enigmatic old man, somewhat demented perhaps, one who at one time had been closely associated with Judah's so-called Christ, now a leader among the Jesus people and therefore a real threat to the emperor and the Empire.

While Patmos guards and officials served a brutal sovereign, they were, after all, human, and most of them manifested some of the better qualities of humanity. Prisoners who were cooperative and nonbelligerent were normally very well treated. Among the privileges allowed them was the freedom to receive items from friends and family elsewhere and to send and receive communications, letters. All these were of course closely examined and either approved or rejected by the Roman censors. They allowed no communication critical of Rome or that in any way appeared to be subversive.

With almost all incoming ships, John received messages from his people at Ephesus and the surrounding area. All these, though, had been guardedly written, and in addition many had been severely censored. As it would be later known, some would never be delivered at all. While he was allowed very little specific information, John received enough to know that the Jesus people in and around Ephesus were suffering greatly under the edicts that continued to come in from Rome. By this, of course, he was greatly troubled.

Upon their request, cooperative prisoners were sometimes allowed papyrus and quill that they might send messages out. This, for lack of interest or skill, few did. John was by far the most prolific writer, often sending letters both to Ephesus and Athens, as well as to others in other places, always using his marvelous literary skills to say a great deal, yet in ways not to disturb the censors.

It was summertime, and although the island terrain was barren and forbidding, most days were warm and bright. Sunsets were often beautiful and sometimes also the eastern sky when aglow with the dawn.

It was the eastern view that John most preferred, for in this direction, many miles away, lay the heaps of lately fallen stones at the ancient temple's site. Much nearer, though, and of much greater concern to him, lay the teeming coastal areas where many of his fellow disciples lived and labored, people whom he knew and loved much. And now, here from his island prison and from the depths of his spirit, he reached out across the sea, striving to touch them in their peril and pain.

High above the eastward island shoreline stood a lone promontory where other prisoners seldom if ever went. To this summit John often found his way and here spent much time in reflection, meditation, and prayer. It seemed that when here his spirit was set free to soar.

John was an old man now, very old when measured by the lifespan typical of his time. Climbing to his place of reverie above the sea was always difficult for him, at times more so than others, yet it was a climb he made almost daily during those two or three summer months until autumn came.

On Patmos it was difficult for the imprisoned to know the time. For most, however, whether the day be Thursday or Sunday made little difference, normally none. But it mattered greatly to John; day by day, from the first day of his incarceration, he avidly followed a calendar that he devised for himself. He passionately desired to know when each new week began, for on each week's first day the followers of Jesus everywhere would be celebrating his resurrection, and John always yearned to be with them.

Thus whenever at all possible, on each Lord's Day morning he made his way to that summit beside the sea and longingly reached in spirit as far as he could toward the shore of Asia Minor.

XIII

On one such morning, as John laboriously picked his way upward amid the lava stones, there came to him with clarity a memory from many years before. It was the memory of another Lord's Day morning, the very first one, when on the supple limbs of youth he had outrun Simon Peter and arrived first at the entrance of an empty tomb. That memory was followed closely by a thought: Christ lives! but Rome rules; when, O when, will the rule of evil ever end and the kingdom of our Lord really come?

Wearily, then, that morning the apostle John was in his accustomed place, facing, as always, eastward. Before him, of course, were the rising sun and all the configurations of the morning sky.

We shall never know precisely what happened next. By what power of discernment are we ever qualified to comprehend the intimate communication between a saint and his God? Perhaps, only perhaps, in John's reaching forth to his friends across the sea, his reach was somewhere intercepted by the reaching hand of God. All we know, though, is that however it came about, there is no doubt that somehow that day the Lord met his apostle in a very singular way.

And no doubt when the man later that day descended from his pinnacle place there must have shown on his countenance such a glow as was seen on the face of Moses when he came down from the Holy Mount. No, John did not bear, as did Moses, two tablets of stone, but in his heart he carried two profound convictions, revelations really.

The first of these was this: In the awful world-shattering contest between good and evil, the good will win in the end. The second was similar to this: Rome the apparently invincible, seeking, as it seemed, to destroy all who followed Christ and worshiped God, Rome, who esteemed herself eternal, would be herself destroyed, and all who suffered her depredations would be free of her at last; as Great Babylon had fallen, so would Rome.

For John, a well-remembered word of Jesus assumed a loftier meaning now. To his disciples Jesus had said, "In the world you will have tribulation, but be of good cheer; I have overcome the world." As John saw it, all human affairs were aspects of the great contest between the all-conquering Christ and all evils of the world, Rome included, and especially Rome.

John was utterly convinced that all disciples could be absolutely sure of this: The living Christ would yet be living long after Rome, like some more recent Babylon, had become only a dismal page on the record books of time. As John saw it, all disciples of Jesus would be greatly comforted and encouraged to know that evil was even then being vanquished, that mighty Rome was going down, and that in the great contest the Lord would be victorious and all his own would share the victory with him.

Immediately, John was moved by a compelling urge to tell everyone about this. His was an impassioned yearning to bring this message of hope to all his imperiled and suffering people; it would mean much to them to receive the good news that had so stirred and inspired him.

But John was in prison. He was not permitted to go to his people nor they to come to him. His only way of reaching them was to write.

However, all outgoing mail being thoroughly scrutinized, nothing critical of Rome was ever allowed to pass. And especially any suggestion that the Roman Empire would one day utterly collapse had absolutely no chance at all. Yet it was this banner headline that John urgently wished to publish to his fellow disciples everywhere. But by what miracle of communication could he ever get his message out?

In the first place, John faced a problem common among all who see visions: how to picture in language the meaning of the vision seen. Perhaps a mystic's vision never comes as a page of neatly numbered squares with clear instruction as to what colors are to be painted in, but rather as a fleeting glimpse of a grand spectacular, requiring many artful brush-strokes to render it visible to another's eye or intelligible to another's mind.

For John, however, the greater problem was the censorship. There was, though, one possible way of dealing with that. Instead of speaking of Rome literally, perhaps he could speak figuratively, perhaps he could write in such a way that Rome would be implied but not identified.

After all, had not the vision itself come in a highly symbolic manner? He had seen and heard it clearly; he had clearly understood the meaning of it; he had no doubt of that. Perhaps another viewer may not have seen in it the same magnificent truths that were so very clear to him. Perhaps, he thought, as the greatest of art can be truly seen only by the prepared and perceptive eye, so may it be with revelations such as this. As he had received a message some other may have missed, perhaps he could now utilize symbolism to bring comfort to Christians and confound Romans.

Why not? For the Hebrew culture, unlike the more practical and pragmatic Roman, had lived and breathed and spoken metaphor for more than two thousand years. For example: God was a shepherd, people were sheep led sometimes by still waters, mountains broke forth into song, Ephraim was a cake only half baked, the sun had stood still over Mount Gilboa.

So, figuratively, what symbol would best represent and identify Rome? Would there be another country, another city? Yes, there would — Babylon and the Babylonian empire. In the Hebrew tradition, from the perspective of Judaism and of Jewish Christians, there was no doubt of it. For almost seven centuries these people had lived, generation after generation, under the dark shadow of the ruin brought on them by that ancient power.

To these who knew their history well, it now appeared that Rome was virtually a resurrected Babylon. As Babylon had once ruled the world, so now did Rome. As Babylon had once destroyed their nation, Rome had now destroyed it once again. Their temple had been utterly destroyed twice, first by Babylon in 586 BC and now by Rome in AD 70. Their people had twice been evicted from their homeland, first taken as captives into Babylon and now dispersed by Rome into the far corners of the world. Most horrendous of it all, even as the Babylonians had mocked Judah's religion and desecrated her sacred instruments, the Romans, so it appeared, were now resolved to destroy both ancient Judaism and her newborn child, Christianity.

The longer John thought of it, the more certain he became that Asian Christians would comprehend and the Roman censors would suspect nothing. His conclusion, then, was this: He would write in code. In code he would proclaim the fall of the Roman empire, and in code he would disclose related aspects of his vision.

XIV

John loved his people, and he knew that they loved and trusted him. He supposed that he would never again see them or ever again visit Ephesus or the other cities of Asia. He was torn with feelings akin to those of the faithful shepherd who is forcibly shut away from his flock when the wolf pack is upon it.

There would, therefore, be an extreme urgency about his writing. What had been revealed to him he would now undertake to reveal to those he so much cared about, and this he felt he must do quickly and clearly. As for the message, his task would be to reveal it and yet conceal it. He would reveal it to some and conceal it from others.

John knew his task to be a great one; it involved two dangers actually. First was the possibility that some censoring official would be more insightful than John had anticipated, and that if his subterfuge were to be discovered, he and others of the faith would be deemed guilty of sedition. The other was that, his work passing their inspection, these officials might later be accused of treason for having passed it.

While John utterly detested the policies of the empire, he felt no animosity toward these government underlings who were simply doing an assigned work. They were, John believed, rather common types of men; they had been reasonably good to him, and he wished to cause them no harm. He looked upon these men as victims of Rome's cruel misuse of power, in some ways even as he and his people were.

For many reasons, John would be under the necessity of writing with extreme care and rare skill. He would therefore disguise his essential truths beneath an overlayer that presumably only the well-informed of his own cultural and religious orientation would be able to peel away.

What John wrote, therefore, was a long convoluted, complicated letter, a book really. He used mysterious images and symbolisms. He painted outlandish pictures gigantic in dimension, scenes so other-worldly as to appear ridiculous. There were hundred-pound hailstones falling to earth, dragon's tails sweeping stars from the sky, the whole sky rolling itself up like a scroll and disappearing, hail and fire mixed with blood, stars falling, and unearthly beasts with bodies nightmarishly grotesque. There were sounds such as great earthquakes make, and thunders, and trumpets talking. And, too, there was a great deal of music, great crescendos of it, and a lot of singing, joyous and triumphant, but on strange themes, unlike any those Romans ever knew.

First, though, he would put a very significant preface in front of all that. He would identify himself, clearly state his relationship with his readers, put himself in a well-defined geographical location, and graphically describe the circumstances under which he would write. I am John, he would say, your brother in the kingdom of Christ and your companion in suffering. He would say: On the island called Patmos, in the spirit, on the Lord's Day, I heard a voice and the voice said, "Write."

So John wrote. He addressed his message to seven churches in Asia. Continuing in the prelude mode, he first gave those churches some practical advice, carefully saying nothing that would stir any Roman suspicions. Finishing with the churches, he then leaped headlong into the message uppermost on his mind.

He wrote that a door opened in heaven. And with the opening of that door would begin a drama unmatched by anything anywhere anytime. That drama would have to do with the future, the future of Rome and of all evil, the future of righteousness and of all disciples of Jesus.

John wrote of a book closed by seven seals that none but one could open. There were seven angels with seven trumpets, each in turn sounding, these followed in turn by a woman clothed with the sun, a beast rising from the sea, and a lamb standing on Mount Zion. He wrote then of seven angels pronouncing judgments upon the evils of the world, the last of which was a judgment against one he named the great whore, with whom the kings of the earth had committed fornication.

This woman was drunk with the blood of the martyred disciples of Jesus, and on her very forehead her identity was clearly written: "Babylon the Great, mother of harlots and abominations of the earth." Later, John declared the great whore to be the great city that reigned over the earth. Later still, he portrayed the grief of her paramours upon seeing the smoke of her burning.

Rome? Yes, certainly; there could be no other. And John was confident that well-informed disciples in Ephesus and elsewhere would understand this.

As John recounted his vision, he pictured a dramatic sequence of scenes. At least six times by name and often otherwise, he threaded in very pointed references to Babylon, always evil, always falling or fallen. Her sins had reached to the heavens, he said; in one hour her judgment had come, and she was going down as a millstone goes when dropped into the sea.

This ascending scenario of destruction reaching culmination at last, John then portrayed Great Babylon utterly thrown down, never to be found at all, and within that city, once great, the light of a candle never again to shine, and the music of trumpeters and harpists and pipers to be heard no more.

But this was not the end of John's report of his vision of the future. He would also write of two episodes specifically offering encouragement and symbols of forthcoming victory to his people everywhere.

First, he would assure his people that in the awesome contest between good and evil the good would be victorious. All the powers of evil were arranged phalanx-like against Christ and his kingdom, solidly entrenched until the ultimate battle would come. In that final struggle all that was anti-Christ would be vanquished forever. And when the awful battle was ended, standing alongside the Christ on the field of victory would be the vast multitude of his people, the called, the chosen, and the faithful. So for the suffering saints of Ephesus and everywhere would come freedom and victory at last.

Second, John would paint into his final scenes the ecstasy of those who were reclaimed from the awful troubles they had gone through. Christ and his people would feast together; there would be music and light and rejoicing always. There would be a new heaven and a new earth. Significantly, there would be a new Jerusalem, so magnificent the old one could never begin to compare at all. Significantly too, there would be no more sea, no sea ever to imprison anyone on any Patmos ever again. And at length Jesus would be acclaimed by his friends and admitted by his enemies to be King of kings and Lord of lords.

And so, John hoped, in all of this his people would find, beyond their present pain, a future to believe in, a triumph to strive for, and the courage to hold fast their faith through whatever Rome and the powers of evil might mass against them. Though his towering truth bore a mysterious camouflage, John was sure his people would understand it — if only it could survive the scrutiny of the Romans who managed affairs from those long, low basalt buildings at the south end of the island.

XV

Rome's island prison was operated and controlled by a small contingent of soldiers. With the Roman military being thinly deployed throughout the vast empire, only a few men could be made available for assignments such as this. Actually, not many were needed on Patmos. Much of the necessary labor was performed by the imprisoned. Furthermore, the island being surrounded as it was by at least thirty miles of open sea, there was little likelihood of an escape, and therefore few men were assigned to guard duty.

The Patmos post, nevertheless, was considered of high importance, and men posted there had been chosen for their loyalty and general competence. None, though, were especially skilled or trained for their specific duties.

Certainly those who checked incoming and outgoing mail had only limited knowledge of the historic and literary, and even less of Hebraic culture and tradition.

While John thought of these men as unfortunates trapped in the claws of Roman power, they saw themselves as servants of it, their primary mission to serve Rome as efficiently as they were able. Most, though, were quite aware of their inadequacies, and none more so than those whose duty it was to determine the fate of communications in transit. Their assignment actually required more expertise than they were qualified to provide.

The Roman standard of justice, although terribly perverted at points, was nevertheless somewhat higher than most such standards had ever been, although sometimes grossly compromised by such despots as Domitian, the one who ruled Rome at the time. Despite the perfidy prevailing in Domitian's empire, many Romans sought diligently to maintain some humane ideals. It was a time of ethical uncertainty and moral ambiguity, and the Romans who served on Patmos were caught in the general confusion of their time. On the one hand, they wished to deal fairly in all matters and on the other to be good servants of the emperor and the Empire.

So it was when John delivered his massive multi-layered letter to the men who would make the official judgment of it. The first man to view it found no problem with it, not at the beginning anyway. Then he reached the point where that door opened in heaven and other-worldly voices began to speak. From here on, John's letter made no sense. To him, all of it appeared to be the ramblings of a failing mind or the illusions of a poetic visionary of the sort whose writings, he believed, never meant anything to anybody anyway. He saw no message in it, no meaning, and no harm really.

This man knew John as a quiet, harmless old man who often wrote letters containing what seemed quaint and innocuous observations about life and religion. Now, here probably was yet another of these, but he was not altogether sure of it.

Uncertain what his decision should be, he took the matter to his centurion, and the two men considered it together. After some discussion, the higher officer at last smiled a little and said, "Let's humor the old man; let it go." And so John's great letter went, and that Roman probably never knew the supreme importance of the decision he made that day.

XVI

How great was the excitement not long thereafter when John's huge letter reached his friends east of the Aegean! It was another Lord's Day morning, not unlike one John had seen on Patmos a few months before, and the sun had just arisen over the hills east of Ephesus. Early, as was their custom, the disciples of Jesus had gathered at one of their meeting places.

Usually at these gatherings, after greetings, there was for a while among the people a mood of remembrance and meditation in which all minds were filled by a spoken or unspoken thought: He lives! Our Lord is risen; He lives! Then normally they shared news and experiences of the week, discussed the issues of their faith and time, prayed, received communications from others, read and studied the ancient scriptures, and comforted and encouraged one another. Today, though, that custom would be significantly interrupted.

Continuing in the mode of reverence, one of the older men stepped forward, carefully placed a mass of parchment on a table, and said to all assembled, "We have a message from our brother John."

Instantly, of course, there was total attention. John's people always awaited any message from him and carefully read and weighed every word. Now here was yet another.

The consideration of John's new message commenced immediately. As one carefully and thoughtfully read, all others intently and thoughtfully listened. Today they heard and clearly understood John's greeting, his identification of himself, and his description of his circumstance.

Then they read of one who had lived, had been dead, and was now alive again forever, and they instantly knew that to fulfill this role only the Lord Jesus could possibly qualify. Further, in his right hand he held seven stars, and these, John said, represented seven of the churches in Asia. Surely, being in his right hand, not his left, these churches must be of great importance to him who holds their stars. So John would relay the Lord's message to those churches, and the people would read this and readily understand and accept it.

Then, suddenly in John's letter the tone changed: A door opened in heaven and a voice was heard speaking. That opening door created a stir among the people. After all, there is always something beyond a door; an opening door is always a revelation. And that voice promised even more: "I will show you what will take place hereafter."

What will take place hereafter? That phrase struck deep chords in almost every heart. These were a people whose prospects for the future were dim and uncertain. The very suggestion that they might know something of their tomorrows was an awesome one. Could anyone ever know? If anyone could, that one would be John; they were confident of that. Was he now about to tell them? They were caught somewhere between hope and fear. What would John say? It was therefore with a breathless anxiety that they watched and listened as the scroll was unrolled and read.

Soon, though, their excitement gave way to consternation. What had been impossible for those Romans to understand now proved difficult also for these disciples. Their lit-up faces quickly overclouded with uncertainty, as anxiously they glanced one to another. What was John saying really? Something very important, no doubt, but what?

From that moment on, during the rest of that day, and during much of many days for several weeks to follow, John's beleaguered flock and their neighbors from all around tried hard to comprehend what their imprisoned shepherd was saying to them.

They would succeed eventually, but only after intensive study and much discussion, utilizing all their knowledge of language and history and of their own cultural and religious heritage. That process would be, from start to finish, a consummate adventure of mind and spirit, sometimes fraught with discouragement and sometimes caught up in the exaltation of eye-opening discovery.

Early on, they discovered that John had painted for them a series of pictures or, perhaps more accurately said, had written for them a series of separate acts in a single majestic drama. There were several of these, sometimes overlaid one with another or blended, and therefore difficult to see, but when seen would stand forth clear and strong.

John had so camouflaged his salient truths that many readers would have given up. But not these people; they knew the author, they knew him well, they were fully confident that he had something important to say to them, and they would search until they found it.

XVII

If we may attempt to trace the path John's people followed to an understanding of his message, we find first of all One seated on a throne. This One is not named, but the scene is clearly painted: There are symbols of enormous power, there are many who adore and worship the enthroned One, and it is said that he created all things and will live forever and ever.

This one is God, no doubt. But why does John not say so? He has always spoken freely of God; why does he avoid it now? There must be a reason, a very compelling one. But what is it?

In God's right hand there is a scroll, a book. This is God's right hand, not his left, and among the many possible and wonderful uses of that hand, he is using it very modestly, simply to hold a book. This book, therefore, John's readers reasoned, must be of high significance. Books are important for what is in them; so what is in this one? They want to know; but no one knows, for the book is sealed, not merely with a single seal but with seven.

A great question arises: Who can open these seals? The answer: No one except a lamb, not some powerful beast like a lion, but a timid young creature, surely not qualified by power of tooth and claw. Besides, this lamb has been slaughtered, previously killed.

Ancibently, for the sins of the people, lambs had been slaughtered on sacrificial altars. More recently, for the sins of the world, Christ had sacrificed himself upon a cross. So, who is this who alone can open the book? Of course, it is quite clear, it will be the Christ, not named by John but casually referred to as the Lamb of God.

Again, the people are asking: Why? Why does John not speak plainly of Christ or of Jesus? The people ponder the question; they really wrestle with it. Then comes the thought: Is John perhaps letting them know right up front that he will identify persons or things not usually by their common names but in some symbolic way? Why, though, would John disguise whatever he wanted them to know? Why would he conceal rather than reveal? It was not in his character to tease or taunt them or to play some cruel game.

Not long afterward, however, all those questions suddenly became a joyous exclamation. The clues John had given his readers were clearly read. They now understood that only by concealing his message from the Romans could he get it through to them and that this he had indeed done.

From this point forward, John's readers would study his message in a brighter illumination, with an elevated level of confidence and in a mood of joyous excitement.

As those seven seals are broken one by one, they reveal a people suffering affliction, persecution, pain. This people is not named, of course, but the disciples clearly see themselves at the center of the picture; they are confident John is speaking of them.

Then the scene changes, and there is awful cataclysm; the earth trembles, the sun is black, the heavens are rolled up like a scroll, and those who have brought horrible suffering upon the disciples are defeated, demolished, completely undone, and in terror they ask the mountains to fall upon them. They will be there never again to hurt or harm the disciples of the Lord.

Again, there is a change of scene, a glorious change, and huge multitudes in white garments stand in adoring attitude before the great throne. Who are these? it is asked. And in answer it is said: "These are they who have come out of the great ordeal, the great affliction." Here at the throne of God they worship with none to hinder them, and here they will never hunger or thirst, and all tears will be wiped away.

These Asian disciples are indeed at this very moment held in the clutches of a terrible ordeal, and they are totally convinced that John is telling them that they will come out of it and go on beyond it. This is the very best of good news for them, but it is awfully difficult to believe. Nevertheless, whatever John foresees they will try their utmost also to see; they trust him. In the bright vistas he paints for them they begin to see the first light of a new hope.

Reading on, they soon discover that his long letter to them is somewhat like a fine symphony. A single theme, variously expressed, is repeated over and over, though sometimes in scenes not altogether beautiful.

So it is with a scenario in which all the evil forces of the earth make war against the Lamb. It is an earth-shattering struggle. Lambs are not usually known as great fighters, but despite the mighty powers arrayed against him, this one wins. And the Lamb has not been alone in the struggle. He has had a loyal following who have stood with him in the fight; these are the called, the chosen, and the faithful. And when the battle is over, the Lamb carries all these away to a magnificent celebration, not unlike a festive wedding, and John names it the Marriage Supper of the Lamb.

John's people understand that it is they who will sit at the great banquet table with their victorious Lord, and they deeply resolve to be always among the faithful. Their prospects for the future become brighter and brighter with each new revelation.

For them, a revelation of supreme importance is the one concerning the downfall of Rome. "Great Babylon is fallen!" That word repeated several times, they readily grasp the meaning of it. Although that meaning had eluded the Patmos censors, it was now obvious to the Ephesian Christians. John had so masterfully designed his symbolisms that the more astute among his friends at Ephesus easily understood that every mention of Babylon was a reference to Rome.

Then comes at length the most horrible of symbolisms: the great whore, drunk with the blood of saints, who has polluted and defiled nations and people everywhere. On her very forehead is clearly written: "Babylon the Great, Mother of Harlots." Then, wasted by her own sins, her infamies ended, she goes down, down, and there arises the smoke of her burning.

So goes Rome and so goes all evil; the reign of the wrong is ended, the Day of the Lord is come, and he shall reign King of kings and Lord of lords. In the momentous contest between good and evil, good has won at last, and the victory is forever.

How firm is now the confidence, how deep the consolation, how strong the faith, and how great the joy of these Christian disciples who have seen so much of suffering and now have seen, beyond an opening door, the wonders of the life that will be theirs!

This, however, is not the end; John has more for them, much more: A new Jerusalem. The old one is gone, destroyed by Romans not long ago. But the new will come and will be the abiding place of all who are wedded to the Lamb. And here there will be no more death, nor sorrow, nor pain.

The new Jerusalem will be infinitely superior to the old one and the very antithesis of old Rome. As Rome will be going down into the dust, the new Jerusalem will be coming down from God out of heaven. John says it plainly: Even a candle will never again burn in fallen Rome, and the light will never go out in the new Jerusalem.

No symbolisms of greater power have ever appeared in human speech or in the scope of human vision, and thanks to John's unparalleled gift, his people heard, saw, and understood.

XVIII

John's message had gotten through, all the way from the depths of one great soul to the grieving, hungry hearts of a beloved people. After many weeks of writing and other weeks of reading, a remarkable venture in communication was brought successfully to conclusion. John had done his work well, and so had his people done theirs.

These people now knew, or believed they did, that all good was on its way upward and onward and all evil was on its way down and out. They now understood that beyond all the sorrows and pangs of pain they felt, a glorious victory somewhere awaited them. They were now convinced that no obstacle could ever be so great that they should let it hinder them. They were totally confident that, though the road be sometimes rough, the destination was worth the journey. Whatever the current circumstances, there would always be something good for them to go on to, and they deeply resolved, most of them anyway, to be always pressing forward, going on.

Had John on Patmos known of his people's great joy, he would have rejoiced greatly also. He did not then know, but later he would, and he and they would rejoice together.

XIX

Writing his letter, John had, of course, reported the vision he had seen from the eastern coast of Patmos on that memorable Lord's Day morning. He had, though, written not merely from what he had lately seen but also from what he had long suspected.

Of course, John had read Plato, and like the apostle Paul, but much more extensively than Paul, had discussed philosophy with the scholars at Mars Hill. He had followed Plato's long quest for the ideal human society and had noted, along with many others, Plato's conclusion that the ideal was unattainable. And why was it unattainable? Because of defects within individual human persons.

Observing Rome and Romans, John had been long convinced that he saw those same defects there. He had, he believed, seen in most Romans of the upper and ruling classes those qualities of character that would one day bring Rome to the brink of ruin.

During the final years of John's lifetime, Rome was ruled by nine different emperors, and of these only two died naturally. There were two suicides and five assassinations; being emperor of Rome was a hazardous occupation. One may reasonably assume that John's Patmos vision did not greatly surprise him, but it was certainly conclusive for him.

Among emperors, Domitian was one of the worst and had continued to grow worse year by year during the fourteen years he ruled. It had been during his final year that John was arrested and taken away to Patmos.

Now comes word from Rome that Domitian is dead, assassinated, and that Nerva will assume the throne. This news reaching Ephesus allowed a collective sigh of relief and an uplifted prayer of thanksgiving. Everyone understands that Nerva is a better man. Soon after comes the news that persecution of Christians will ease somewhat.

No, official Rome has not suddenly embraced Christianity, but Rome has become aware of what best serves her self-interest. Nerva well understands that outlawing Christianity has not slowed its growth or solved anything. Officials have found it terribly difficult to enforce the laws against the Jesus people. They have also found maintenance of their many prisons quite expensive and a drain on manpower. Thus, for practical reasons, the decision is made to close the Patmos facility and release most inmates.

With reception of this news, there is much rejoicing among Jesus people everywhere, especially in Ephesus. Here a wellspring of hope arises and flows mightily in every heart: The people fondly hope they will see John again, perhaps soon. He has now been imprisoned about a year and a half altogether – most of one summer, all of one winter and the following summer, and now well into the second winter. Now he may be coming home.

XX

The harbor at Ephesus lay under the pall of a dreary winter day. There was enough wind to stir the water, and modest whitecaps could be seen here and there. At dockside two or three small ships rocked on uneven waves and made occasional scraping sounds against the mooring posts. Unlike the spring, when everything seems young, today all aspects of nature seemed to speak of the aged and the worn.

On the dock, warmly wrapped against the chill, stood a cluster of men and a few women, all of them as one facing westward, gazing intently toward the open sea. Soon, against the dim horizon, the topmost rigging of a ship appeared, moving eastward.

A wave of excitement momentarily overswept the clustered group, and then all were quiet again, facing westward as before. All were soon aware, from the movements of the vessel, that she was coming in. As she drew nearer and was more clearly seen, she appeared to be a large, dark ship of the class that normally moved back and forth between Ephesus and Patmos, a supply and transport vessel. Again, a wave of excitement swept over the group assembled there.

Later, as seamen wrestled with wayward sails, easing their ship toward the dock, it was seen that she bore as her ensign the proud and often feared Roman Eagle. To those waiting it now appeared certain: This would be the ship on which John would be coming home.

Indeed it was, and not only John but also a virtual shipload of others, mostly disciples and a number of these of the Ephesian fellowship.

As disembarking began, there were occasional greetings and sometimes expressions of joy as friends and acquaintances met and recognized one another. Such moments of fraternity, however, were actually more an interruption than a main interest among those who had come to meet the incoming vessel. Their interest was in the arrival of John, which they believed would occur today, and they constantly searched the gunwales for any sight of him.

At length he appeared, much older it seemed to them than when they had seen him last. Two younger men, disciples obviously, stood with him, and with supreme care were attending him. Assisted by these, the apostle moved forward, unsteadily but clearly trying to stand as tall as waning strength would allow.

As he reached the dock, his Ephesian friends rushed forward, surrounding him but standing back apace, awestruck. For a moment that seemed longer than it really was, no one spoke, and no one reached forth to touch him.

Later, some older men who stood nearest would say that although he seemed terribly weak and tired, there was in his eyes that same far-seeing light they had first observed more than thirty years before, a light as though lit by the beams from some distant star.

It was a high moment of respect and adoration. They are rare, but there are sometimes silences so laden with feeling that it would be an intrusion to break them with speech, and this was one of those. Deeply, all the people felt it.

But time for speech would come, and did. The oldest of the elders spoke: "Welcome home, Brother John, welcome home."

Even the youngest present would never forget John's reply. His voice strong despite the tremor of age that was in it, John smiled and said, "Thank you, thank you for the welcome — but not home really, not quite — just a pleasant pause in passing — I shall soon be going on."

www.ingramcontent.com/pod-product-compliance
Lightning Source LLC
Chambersburg PA
CBHW071344130626
46556CB00005B/2021